Acting Edition

Faculty Portrait

by Sean David DeMers

FOR PRODUCTION INQUIRIES

UNITED STATES AND CANADA
info@concordtheatricals.com
1-866-979-0447

UNITED KINGDOM AND EUROPE
licensing@concordtheatricals.co.uk
020-7054-7298

Each title is subject to availability from Concord Theatricals Corp.,
depending upon country of performance. Please be aware that
FACULTY PORTRAIT may not be licensed by Concord Theatricals
Corp. in your territory. Professional and amateur producers should
contact the nearest Concord Theatricals Corp. office or licensing
partner to verify availability.

No one shall make any changes in this title(s) for the purpose of production. No part of this book may be reproduced, stored in a retrieval system, scanned, uploaded, or transmitted in any form, by any means, now known or yet to be invented, including mechanical, electronic, digital, photocopying, recording, videotaping, or otherwise, without the prior written permission of the publisher. No one shall share this title(s), or any part of this title(s), through any social media or file hosting websites.

For all inquiries regarding motion picture, television, online/digital and other media rights, please contact Concord Theatricals Corp.

MUSIC AND THIRD-PARTY MATERIALS USE NOTE

Licensees are solely responsible for obtaining formal written permission from copyright owners to use copyrighted music and/or other copyrighted third-party materials (e.g. artworks, logos) in the performance of this play and are strongly cautioned to do so. If no such permission is obtained by the licensee, then the licensee must use only original music and materials that the licensee owns and controls. Licensees are solely responsible and liable for clearances of all third-party copyrighted materials, including without limitation music, and shall indemnify the copyright owners of the play(s) and their licensing agent, Concord Theatricals Corp., against any costs, expenses, losses and liabilities arising from the use of such copyrighted third-party materials by licensees. For music, please contact the appropriate music licensing authority in your territory for the rights to any incidental music.

IMPORTANT BILLING AND CREDIT REQUIREMENTS

If you have obtained performance rights to this title, please refer to your licensing agreement for important billing and credit requirements.

FACULTY PORTRAIT was first produced in 2015 at the University of Iowa's MFA New Play Festival in Iowa City, Iowa. The play was directed by Ariel Francoeur assisted by Caitlin Dorsett, with set design by Cassie Malmquist, lighting design by Ray Ockenfels, costume design by Nicole Ooi and Morgan Meier, original music by Justin Comer, and dramaturgy by Lukas Brasherfons. The production stage manager was Rachel Winfield, and the assistant stage manager was Nic Steffes. The cast was as follows:

CLAIRE	Haley Courter
JAMIE J.	Sasha Hildebrand
MR. Y	Tim Budd
KYLE	Adam Phillips
HELEN	Rubina Vidal
AMY	Taylor Edelle Stuart

FACULTY PORTRAIT was subsequently produced in 2018 and 2019 by Larkin Fine Arts Department at Larkin High School and at the Illinois High School Theater Festival. The play was directed by Frank Rose, with set design by Frank Rose, lighting design by Rebecca Peterson, costumes by Jeremiah Hubbard and Delaney Newman, and original music by Justin Comer. The production stage manager was Ivanna Kurywczak. The cast was as follows:

CLAIRE	Allie Dulabaum
JAMIE J.	Marteena Duckins
MR. Y	Zachary Bohrer
KYLE	Juwan Lockhart
HELEN	Hannah Weber
AMY	Reagan Sanchez
VOICE	Jordan Kosin

FACULTY PORTRAIT was produced in 2020 by Prime Number Productions at IRT Theatre in New York, NY. The play was directed by Ariel Francoeur, with set design by Molly C. Carroll, lighting and projection design by Heather Crocker, costumes by Margaret Gorrell, and dramaturgy by Fiona Kyle. The production stage manager was Shay Thomas. The cast was as follows:

CLAIRE . . . . Phoebe Holden

JAMIE J. . . . . Julie Thaxter-Gourlay

MR. Y . . . . Russ Cusick

KYLE . . . . Shammah "Speed" Waller

HELEN . . . . Molly Schenkenberger

AMY . . . . Jessica Nesi

VOICE . . . . Haley Courter

UNDERSTUDY . . . . Rubina Vidal

CHARACTERS

CLAIRE – Female, Student, 18

JAMIE J – Female, Custodian, Mid 30s

MR. Y – Male, Teacher, Late 40s

KYLE – Male, Student, 18

HELEN – Female, Student, 18

AMY – Female, Student, 18

VOICE – Female

SETTING

A High School building.

TIME

The day before, the day of, and a year later.

AUTHOR'S NOTES

Because of the heavy events and themes of the play there can be a tendency to go toward the darkness and traumatic stress inherent in the characters. Please remember that the ultimate final goal of the play is to be uplifting and optimistic. Keep in mind the strength that it takes these characters to stay in a place surrounded by horrible memories and the desire they have to replace the terrible with the beautiful.

An intermission if required should go after Scene Six.

There is a decent amount of cursing in the show and if you happen to be a company that has to omit these, please consider replacements instead of cuts. This could be in the form of "softer" curse words (but NEVER anything derogatory or aimed at a group of people – amongst others the "b" word and SOB are just not acceptable to me) or perhaps "bleeping" out the curses so we know they are there.

NOTES ON TEXT

(/) – The next character's line starts and overlaps after this symbol.

Scene Number/Time Designation – In previous productions, projecting these for the audience worked well. Feel free to experiment.

for:

*Christoph, Robert, Linhua, Dwight, T. Anne, Rachel, Daniel, William,
Kyle, Steven, Cassie, Isaiah, Matthew, Lauren, John, Kelly, Daniel,
Corey, Emily, Ryan, Ross, Jamie, Brian, Austin, Jocelyn, Daniel, Kevin,
Matthew, Caitlin, Jeremy, Rachael, Matthew, Jarrett, Henry, Liviu,
G.V., Partahi, Lauren, Daniel, Juan, Minal, Erin, Michael, Julia, Mary,
Reema, Waleed, Leslie, Maxine, Nicole, Dawn, Mary, Lauren, Rachel,
Jesse, Victoria, Anne Marie, Dylan, Charlotte, Daniel, Olivia, Josephine,
Ana, Chase, Catherine, Madeline, James, Grace, Noah, Jack, Emilie,
Jessica, Avielle, Alison, Caroline, Benjamin, Araceli, Randy, Mike, Rosie,
Robert, Clarence, Scott, Faye, Randall, Kelly, James, Heather, Chester,
Damon, Tomeka, Karen, Ron, Alejandro, Howard, John, Margaret,
Robert, Judy, Jason, Beamon, Galen, Nacunan, Deanna, Marvin,
Dale, Joseph, Neal, Richard, Robin, Pete, Joey, Carolyn, Diane, Arnold,
Manuel, Leona, Chen, Constantinos, O. Preston, Stephen, Melanie, Josh,
Ron, Mary, Lydia, Christina, Johnpierre, Nicole, Jessica, Kayce, Natalie,
Paige, Stephanie, Britthney, Shannon, John, Robert, William, Faith,
Ben, Mikael, Andrzej, Kayla, Barry, Bryan, Randy, Neal, Robin, Cheryl,
Barbara, Eugene, Norman, Seth, Aaron, Daryl, Michelle, Derrick, Neva,
Alicia, Thurlene, Chanelle, Chase, Dewayne, Jeffrey, Gary, Linda,
Mary, Emily, John, Naomi, Marian, Anna Mae, Lena, Mary, Samnang,
Karsheika, Taniesha, Larry, Catalina, Julianna, Ryanne, Daniel,
Gayle, Omero, Christopher, Ryan, Chavares, Amanda, Justin, Todd,
Gopi, Maria, Adriel, Jose, Vicki, Sam, Ruben, Tremaine, Daniel, Russell,
Demetrius, Tshering, Doris, Sonam, Grace, Katleen, Judith, Lydia,
Gil, Kristopher, Taylor, Tyrone, Samir, Christopher, Carlos, Marcela,
Margarita, Roderick, Michael, Claire, Andrew, Darryl, Cheng, George,
David, Katherine, Veronika, Christopher, Kim, Mark, Ken, Genevieve,
Helene, Nathalie, Barbara, Anne-Marie, Maud, Maryse, Sonia, Michele,
Anne-Marie, Maryse, Annie, Barbara, Annie, Michael, Jaan, Phoivos,
Matthew, Jason, Aysegul, Anastasia, Paul, et al.*

1

The day of

(Exterior of a school building, a window ledge large enough to sit on. Two floors up. Brick. Tall windows. The suggestion of a roof with eaves that overhang the tops of the windows.)

*(**CLAIRE** sits and smokes a cigarette. She seems to be contemplating the meaning of it all when a ladder rises from below to the side of the ledge. She is interested, but not particularly impressed. She continues to smoke.)*

*(Up the ladder comes a custodian, **JAMIE J.** She doesn't really seem to be paying **CLAIRE** much attention.)*

CLAIRE. Hi Jamie J.

JAMIE J. Oh. Hey there.

CLAIRE. Have you come to rescue me?

JAMIE J. Do you need to be rescued?

CLAIRE. I do. I need to be.

JAMIE J. You could climb down the ladder here.

CLAIRE. Is this some kind of reverse psychology?

JAMIE J. What do you mean?

CLAIRE. Maybe someone ratted me out and you're here to get me down and when I get to the bottom of the ladder, Principal Mays will be there with a suspension form. Is that right?

JAMIE J. I don't think so.

CLAIRE. I'll leave by the window, but thanks for the offer.

JAMIE J. Sure.

(*She is trying to ignore* **CLAIRE.** *She's looking at the eaves.*)

CLAIRE. Guess how long I've been doin' this.

JAMIE J. Well I looked up here ten minutes ago, so I'd say less than that.

CLAIRE. I mean overall. Cumulatively. Guess how long cumulatively I've been sneakin' out here.

JAMIE J. Listen, I don't like guessing and I get the feeling you're gonna tell me anyway.

CLAIRE. Sophomore year. Two years. Only ever seen one other person. Have you seen me up here before?

JAMIE J. Nope.

CLAIRE. Nope. HERE I AM WORLD!

Okay, I give up. What are you up here for if not to get me down?

JAMIE J. Gotta get the hornet's nest.

CLAIRE. What hornet's nest?

(*She follows* **JAMIE J**'s *gaze.*)

Oh. *That* hornet's nest.

JAMIE J. Yup.

CLAIRE. I never noticed it.

JAMIE J. Easy to miss. Only been here a couple weeks. Look, it's not even done yet.

CLAIRE. Where's your equipment?

JAMIE J. What do you mean?

CLAIRE. Do you have a stick, or a hose, or a gun?

JAMIE J. A gun?

CLAIRE. Like a water hose with a spray gun. Or maybe you can poison them, or fog them out?

JAMIE J. I'm just weighing my options.

CLAIRE. Oh. You want a cig?

(**JAMIE J** *surreptitiously looks around.*)

JAMIE J. I don't know. Whatya got?

CLAIRE. The cheapest I can get.

(*She hands* **JAMIE J** *a cigarette and a lighter.* **JAMIE J** *inhales.*)

JAMIE J. Mmm. These really suck.

CLAIRE. Yeah, but cheap.

(**JAMIE J** *takes in the scenery.*)

JAMIE J. It's nice up here. We gonna get busted?

CLAIRE. Room's empty this period.

JAMIE J. Mr. Y's classroom?

CLAIRE. Yeah. He's nice.

JAMIE J. One of the few teachers that talk to me.

CLAIRE. Cool. I found out yesterday he used to be a smoker.

JAMIE J. You don't say. They don't bother you?

CLAIRE. At first I thought this was the perfect spot and maybe someone would see me and I would be known as the cool smoker, but actually it's a little lame to sit on a ledge outside the window of a classroom. Turns out no one wants to bother me.

JAMIE J. I was talking about the hornets.

CLAIRE. Include them as part of "no one."

JAMIE J. Ah.

CLAIRE. Are you gonna knock the nest down when I go in?

JAMIE J. Haven't decided what to do. Probably try from inside. I don't want that thing landing on me out here. Whatever it is, it's gotta be clean. One fell swoop. You don't want to go around poking nests. That just gets 'em angry and then they're all over the place swarming and nasty. You gotta take it out in one shot so the whole thing falls to the ground, explodes, and they run off to find a new home. I'm thinking I could just get a long stick and lean out this window.

CLAIRE. Nope. Gotta do that window.

JAMIE J. Wouldn't work, this one's the only angle.

CLAIRE. Yeah, but it sticks. I always gotta use the other one.

JAMIE J. Since when does it stick?

> (**JAMIE J** *gets up and tries it out. It sure does stick.*)

CLAIRE. At least since I was a sophomore.

JAMIE J. You shoulda told someone. We could fix it.

CLAIRE. Jamie J?

JAMIE J. Yeah?

CLAIRE. This window sticks. Could you fix it?

JAMIE J. Alright smartass, I'll put it on the list.

CLAIRE. The list?

JAMIE J. There's a lot of priorities, we gotta rank 'em.

CLAIRE. Where would this rank?

JAMIE J. Probably dead last.

CLAIRE. Great.

(**CLAIRE** *gets up and goes to the window.*)

Jamie –

JAMIE J. Hm?

CLAIRE. Have you ever told someone the truth about something and you thought it would make everything better, but you felt worse?

JAMIE J. ...

CLAIRE. Nevermind. You should do this after school when no one's around.

JAMIE J. Hey, thanks for the smoke – and the new smoking section. You don't mind if I use it?

CLAIRE. Nope. I got another one on the roof.

(*She is gone.*)

2

A year later

(The interior of Mr. Y's classroom. Afterschool.
MR. Y *is sitting behind a desk grading papers.*
KYLE *sits at a desk reading a book.)*

KYLE. Hey, Mr. Y?

(No response.)

Mr. Y? Since there's like, no one else here, could we cancel detention?

MR. Y. No.

KYLE. But I'm missing practice. What if I make it up like, tomorrow or something?

MR. Y. I'm not coming in here on a Saturday.

KYLE. Why do we have to be in *this* room?

MR. Y. It's my classroom – just go back to reading quietly.

KYLE. Mr. Y, have you seriously read the *Iliad*?

MR. Y. Multiple times.

KYLE. No offense, but I find that hard to believe. I can't read this anymore.

MR. Y. You should've thought of that before you pulled Maria's bra strap.

KYLE. I couldn't resist.

MR. Y. You have to learn to resist, Kyle. That's why you're here.

KYLE. I thought I was here 'cause I'm a pervert.

MR. Y. No.

KYLE. You don't think I'm a pervert? Maria called me a pervert in front of everybody! Actually it was awesome – they all laughed – I'm totally a pervert.

MR. Y. You're not a pervert, you're a teenager.

KYLE. Same diff.

MR. Y. No, Kyle. You don't respect people – in this case it was Maria, but in general you've developed a troubling disdain for the world this past year.

KYLE. Haven't we all?

MR. Y. No. You don't have to be a jerk / to everyone.

KYLE. Hey!

MR. Y. I've noticed this pattern escalate and the Maria incident / takes the cake.

KYLE. "Maria incident."

MR. Y. You don't understand how your actions affect other people. Impulses start in your brain and then fire up into ideas, but they don't need to be actions. You have to think before crossing the impulse point.

KYLE. Oh my god, Mr. Y, you didn't see it, it was like all lumpy under her sweater and your lecture was so fucking / boring and –

MR. Y. Don't swear, Kyle.

KYLE. It was *frigging* boring Mr. Y, like even Stewart was asleep and he never falls asleep in your class. He wants to be you – or something.

MR. Y. I didn't notice.

KYLE. Are you fuuu (*A look from* **MR. Y**.) kidding me, you didn't notice? He's like usually asking tons of questions and always has the answers to the quizzes. He's like a mini Mr. Y.

MR. Y. Maybe he's genuinely interested.

KYLE. That's what I'm saying! He usually is, but this time he was asleep and you were saying some shit / about Achilles at the ships –

MR. Y. Kyle seriously, I'll bring you afterschool again.

KYLE. Okay, but you know it's afterschool hours and I hold the swear words in all day. I mean, have you ever heard me say fuck before?

MR. Y. No.

KYLE. Exactly. I'm an afternoon swearer, 'cause I can't do it at home either, but when it's like three p.m. I'm like f-this and f-that and you're an m-er f-er, you f, so f-u! Like that, so really if I swear right now it's your fault for keeping me after.

MR. Y. You swear like this around your coach?

KYLE. He's worse than me! He's taught me some swear words, I mean, my brain can't even comprehend the insult you know? You want to hear a couple?

MR. Y. What do you think?

KYLE. Probably not?

MR. Y. Correct. Read.

KYLE. I just thought this EPIC story about WAR and BATTLES would keep my attention, you know?

MR. Y. *(Lecture mode.)* Homer's characters spanned a range from gods to humans. The mythological to the historical. The author credited with writing two of the finest epic works in the recorded history of the Western world did so / around three thousand years ago –

KYLE. Alright! Shh. I'm reading already.

> *(After a moment,* **MR. Y** *goes to the window. He pulls a sock out of his pocket and contemplates it.)*

*(This puzzles **KYLE** who sneaks an iPhone out and surreptitiously takes **MR. Y**'s picture – for good measure, he also takes a selfie with **MR. Y** in the background. He puts the phone away.)*

You know Mr. Y, this is usually the point in the movie where the teacher feels bad for keeping a healthy student inside on a beautiful day and lets him go early.

MR. Y. It's been twenty minutes.

KYLE. Oh my god, it's forever.

MR. Y. What do you know about forever? Forever is in the eye of the beholder. For you twenty minutes is torture, but what of twenty minutes in the life of a person for whom time has no measure, who is constantly searching – always looking, never finding – traveling through shimmering heat haze and torrential rain. Faces change so often they blur, and names known for ages no longer have meaning to the point he's forgotten his own. Do you know what he's looking for?

KYLE. His name?

MR. Y. Revenge. Cold-blooded revenge so pure even the very emotions are irrelevant, consumed – the blood is clean and strong that pours through the veins and feeds the furnace of the heart.

Dazzling. Diamond studded and razor sharp from the top of the head to the heel, to the soul – the body becomes a weapon. But you see, when the drive for revenge is gone so is that focus, "he that fights fares no better than he that does not;" there is nothing to live for.

KYLE. Are you talking about Achilles?

MR. Y. Yes. Achilles, the greatest soldier in the history of Greece. Why doesn't he leave?

KYLE. It would be a huge f-u to the rest of the army.

MR. Y. Who have only surrounded him with bad memories. He could start over, leave the war behind – I mean, he's on the shore with the ships – he could easily shove off and forget about everything.

KYLE. It's giving up. He wouldn't be a hero.

MR. Y. Achilles believes "coward and hero are held in equal honor" – he doesn't think of himself as a hero.

KYLE. Of course he does! He knows he's the best fighter. They're doomed without him.

MR. Y. But he's still playing with the lives of others. It's a fine line between selfless and selfish.

KYLE. He's making a point. Maybe he stays not just to be a hero, but for everyone – all of the Greeks.

MR. Y. What if he thinks it's for everyone, but it's really only for himself?

> *(Beat. A bang on the door. They jump noticeably. It's **JAMIE J**.)*

Yes?

JAMIE J. Gotta poke a hive.

MR. Y. Does it have to be right now, Jamie?

JAMIE J. It's top of the list, right outside your window. Won't take a minute.

MR. Y. Fine. Come in.

> *(**JAMIE J** enters with a long pole, maybe a broom handle.)*

KYLE. Yo! Jamie J! What a surprise!

JAMIE J. Hey Kyle.

KYLE. Nice stick!

JAMIE J. Gotta / poke a hive.

MR. Y. Kyle, leave her alone.

(**HELEN** *enters.*)

HELEN. Mr. Y, is this a bad time for the faculty portrait?

MR. Y. What? Oh. Right. The yearbook thing.

HELEN. Did you forget?

MR. Y. / Not entirely.

KYLE. He forgot. And he's busy, so beat it.

HELEN. Mind your own business, Kyle.

MR. Y. I have detention for another thirty minutes, it's a little inconvenient now –

HELEN. It's not my fault Kyle got in trouble, why should I be punished?

MR. Y. You really can't come back?

HELEN. The faculty portrait has to be in by Monday morning at the latest. And honestly, you've been kinda blowing me off so – sorry, not sorry.

(**HELEN** *sits behind Mr. Y's desk.*)

MR. Y. Alright –

(**AMY** *enters with a camera. They all look at her.*)

KYLE. Amy too?! This party just got super awkward Mr. Y.

HELEN. Kyle, / grow up!

MR. Y. Just pretend we're not here Kyle.

KYLE. So impossible Mr. Y. Maybe I should just come back.

(**KYLE** *begins packing up.*)

MR. Y. Nice try. Sit.

(**KYLE** *sits.*)

MR. Y. Helen, I thought this was just an interview.

HELEN. Oh, Amy's just gonna shoot – take some pictures.

MR. Y. Can we just do the interview? Maybe use my yearbook photo?

HELEN. It's a bigger spread! We need some candids, it's how we always do it.

MR. Y. We could take them somewhere else. It doesn't have to be in my room. Amy, you don't have to be in here.

HELEN. It's key, Mr. Y. Plus, she wants to.

MR. Y. Amy, you're alright with this?

(She nods with only the barest commitment.)

You don't have to do this for any reason. You can walk away. We'll do it another time, somewhere else.

HELEN. She told me that every room is like every other room.

(MR. Y *looks at* **AMY.** *She nods again.)*

MR. Y. Let's get it over with.

(AMY *places the tape recorder on the desk.)*

HELEN. Oh! I almost forgot, Amy found the tape recorder –

(She stops as **AMY** *flips the tape over and then goes somewhere to set up the camera.)*

Do you mind if I record this?

MR. Y. No.   **KYLE.** Yes!

MR. Y. Kyle –

KYLE. Seriously, Mr. Y? You never know where a recording's gonna end up now, you know?

HELEN. This recording is just for my reference. I'm not gonna post it online or anything.

KYLE. So she says.

MR. Y. Kyle. Read.

KYLE. Sheesh, I'm just trying to protect you. Remember when they posted that stuff you said on that blog? And that depressing picture? They took everything out of context and it could happen again.

MR. Y. Kyle –

KYLE. This is the same thing.

HELEN. It's not the same thing! You were digging that stuff up online, you were obsessed!

KYLE. Right, because someone had to be. You shouldn't trust anyone, Mr. Y – not even Helen.

MR. Y. / Kyle, stop it.

HELEN. Please.

KYLE. Especially not Helen.

HELEN. You're a real piece of work.

KYLE. This is not about me; I'm trying to stop Mr. Y from his impulses. We talked about it earlier.

MR. Y. You're trying to get out of detention. I'm adding ten minutes to this afternoon.

KYLE. Oh, come on!

MR. Y. If you don't shut it, I'll make it more.

(**KYLE** *goes back to reading in a huff.*)

HELEN. I won't use this recording except as a reference when I write the yearbook section, I promise.

MR. Y. I don't care what you do with it. Can we just get started?

HELEN. *(Writing.)* Yes. Mr. Y. Could you spell your last name?

MR. Y. No.

HELEN. Even *you* can't spell it?

MR. Y. I want to be Mr. Y in the yearbook. Like every year.

HELEN. I could just look it up.

MR. Y. I'd rather you didn't.

HELEN. Noted. I've got eight questions. First question: When did you start here?

MR. Y. Twenty years ago.

HELEN. Cool. I wasn't born yet.

MR. Y. None of you were.

HELEN. Well, except for Jamie J.

MR. Y. No, I was talking / about –

JAMIE J. What?!

HELEN. Nothing Jamie.

JAMIE J. Alrighty.

> (**JAMIE J** *goes back to working with her headphones in.*)

> (*This exchange interests* **AMY** *and she begins taking pictures of* **JAMIE J** *at the window.*)

MR. Y. I was referring to the students.

HELEN. I mean, she never actually graduated, so technically JJ's like an eternal / student –

JAMIE J. What?!

HELEN. Nothing Jamie.

JAMIE J. Alrighty.

MR. Y. She has her GED.

HELEN. She does?

KYLE. She does? Really?

MR. Y. Yes, she does.

HELEN. Cool. I didn't know that.

KYLE. Awesome Jamie!

JAMIE J. What?!

KYLE. Sorry, JJ, nothing. Just, congrats on getting your GED!

(*Awkward pause as everyone looks at* **JAMIE J** *and* **AMY** *snaps a picture.*)

(**JAMIE J** *looks to* **MR. Y** *and he shrugs.*)

JAMIE J. Gotta get that damn stuck window open first anyway.

(*She leaves.*)

MR. Y. So, I've been here a while.

(**AMY** *continues taking pictures of the window.*)

HELEN. Cool. Question Two: What was your first day like?

MR. Y. Like any other day.

HELEN. Details Mr. Y, details.

MR. Y. I don't know, I guess it was what you might expect. I was nervous, right out of college. The faculty lounge was quiet. The coffee was terrible, but I had some anyway. The other teachers sat there, contemplating their last moments of freedom. At first, no one said a word to me. And then Mr. Daugherty walked in and made a beeline for me. Fresh blood, I guess.

HELEN. Mr. Doc has been an awesome replacement principal; I interviewed him last year for the portrait.

MR. Y. Of course. I forgot. Last year was supposed to be his final –

HELEN. He even had a retirement party –

KYLE. Helen!

MR. Y. Yeah. He did.

> *(Pause.)*

HELEN. Anyway, Mr. Doc came into the lounge?

MR. Y. What?

HELEN. On your first day?

MR. Y. Oh. Right. Came right at me and I swear the room brightened – he has that effect as you know. He had his own coffee, plopped down next to me and said "Didn't someone warn you not to drink that *(Looks at* **KYLE.***)* crap."

KYLE. There's no way Principal Doc said "crap"!

MR. Y. It's for the yearbook Kyle.

KYLE. / Jeez.

> *(***MR. Y*** points at the book, á la: "back to reading.")*

HELEN. *(Ignoring* **KYLE.***)* What did you say?

MR. Y. Just introduced myself. Doc told me the story of his first day.

HELEN. I can't imagine Principal Doc as a young teacher.

MR. Y. Oh, he was never young. He was born an old man.

KYLE. I'll never get that image out of my head.

> *(***MR. Y*** points at the book again.)*

MR. Y. On his first day here, he met his future wife.

HELEN. What?! He told me last year he couldn't remember.

MR. Y. They met in this very room. It used to be his.

HELEN. This is so great! His wife worked here like Mrs. Y!

(*Pause.*)

Ugh. Sorry. What happened?

MR. Y. It's really his story, I couldn't –

HELEN. Please, Mr. Y? Just tell it. I won't use it on your portrait.

(*Pause.*)

(**AMY** *takes a picture.*)

MR. Y. Well, Mr. Doc walked in and the students were all sitting quietly, facing the front – I guess it truly was a different time then –

KYLE. Very funny.

HELEN. Shush!

MR. Y. So Doc said "It smells chalky in here, dontcha think?" A couple of chuckles and as one of the students leaned out the window to clap erasers, a secretary from the office came in with morning announcements. She put them on his desk and when he looked up at her she said: "I'm Paula from the office, here are the school announcements for you to share. If you need anything just let me know." Doc was taken immediately. He couldn't respond. He smiled. She smiled, turned away, and when she got to the doorway turned back and said: "It smells chalky in here, dontcha think?"

(*They all turn to the doorway. Silence.*)

(**JAMIE J** *bursts through the door loudly with a metal toolbox and drops a crowbar, they all jump and gasp, perhaps a brief scream from* **HELEN.**)

(**AMY** *settles into a crouch near the door.*)

(**JAMIE J** *freezes and then realizes her carelessness.*)

JAMIE J. Sorry. Just. Sorry.

(*She heads to the window and eventually goes out to the ledge.*)

HELEN. That's a nice story.

MR. Y. They're still together. He could've taught anywhere but he never left and, in fact, is probably the only thing holding this building up.

HELEN. Well, you and him.

MR. Y. Everyone who stayed.

HELEN. Did his story make you feel less nervous on your first day?

MR. Y. All day I was waiting for a secretary from the office to come in and sweep me off my feet. Maybe that's why –

HELEN. Why what?

MR. Y. Nothing.

HELEN. Okay. To be continued.

(*She jots a final note down.*)

Question Three: What's your favorite song?

KYLE. Time for the fluff questions. Favorite song, favorite movie, favorite book –

MR. Y. The fluff questions are the best questions.

3

The day of

(The window ledge.)

*(The ladder is there and **JAMIE J** is on the ledge with a stick. She wears headphones, maybe we only hear what she hears and the scene below is a dumbshow or muted.)*

(She looks up at the nest and tries to measure the angle before poking it down.)

(The faint sound of gunshots, two, very muffled.)

*(**JAMIE J** gets a sting on the back of her neck. She thinks of swatting, but instead waves away the hornet. She places the stick on the ledge and takes off a glove to rub the sting.)*

(Another shot, closer.)

CLAIRE. *(Offstage.)* Mrs. Y!

*(**JAMIE J** looks in the classroom.)*

JAMIE J. Claire?

*(**CLAIRE** runs to the closed window and tries to raise it, but it's stuck. **CLAIRE** turns.)*

CLAIRE. Don't do this, please...

(Loud gunshot.)

*(**CLAIRE** falls.)*

JAMIE J. No!

(**JAMIE J** *cringes.*)

(*A final gunshot.*)

(*Transition.*)

4

The day before

(The other side of the school.)

*(**CLAIRE** on the rooftop.)*

*(**AMY** enters.)*

AMY. Are you coming down?

CLAIRE. No.

AMY. You have to eventually.

CLAIRE. I don't.

AMY. Someday.

CLAIRE. Nope, I really don't. I could stay up here forever and no one would miss me.

AMY. Your mom would miss you.

CLAIRE. After a couple days maybe.

AMY. I'd miss you.

CLAIRE. Sure; just not publicly.

AMY. Ugh. Shut up.

CLAIRE. Just go if you're going.

AMY. I hate it up here.

CLAIRE. Great. That makes it easier for you to turn right back around.

AMY. Why don't you just tell me what happened?

CLAIRE. I want to be alone!

AMY. You don't have to be.

CLAIRE. Jesus, do you think I'm gonna jump off the building / or something?

AMY. Well, you were talking to Tim and then you blew me off like a jerk and snuck up to the roof, so what am / I supposed to think?

CLAIRE. You don't have to act all responsible for me.

AMY. No? Then who will?

I'm worried about you.

CLAIRE. Just because I want to be alone doesn't mean it's a big deal, or that I even care about it. It just means I want to be alone!

AMY. I love you.

CLAIRE. Oh my fucking god! You don't! Leave me alone! I don't love you, alright?

(**AMY** *goes to the edge of the roof.*)

AMY. Do you mean that?

CLAIRE. No.

AMY. Would you come down if I jumped?

CLAIRE. It's two stories, you'd just break a leg.

AMY. I'd land on my head. I could jump off right now and be a mystery. Why did she do it? She was so happy with good grades and good friends. So young. So pretty. So talented.

CLAIRE. They wouldn't say any of those things.

(**CLAIRE** *comes up behind* **AMY** *and embraces her.*)

AMY. They would. They'd say them even if they didn't mean them. Say them even if they were lies. Right on the front page with a picture of my last yearbook photo.

CLAIRE. Such a shitty photo.

AMY. Ugh, you're right.

(**CLAIRE** *guides her away from the edge.*)

CLAIRE. Another suicide averted.

AMY. Why won't you just come down?

CLAIRE. This is where I come to think and if you have to know, Tim loves me okay?

AMY. What? He doesn't.

CLAIRE. He said he loves me and he's always loved me and he wants to take me to the fucking prom.

AMY. Oh. What did you tell him?

CLAIRE. Oh my god, don't worry okay? I kept our stupid secret.

AMY. You're gonna go with him?

CLAIRE. What? No, that's what I'm – that's why I'm – ugh, do you see? Keeping this secret is hurting me more than it's protecting us. And now I have to hurt other people too.

AMY. Don't blame me, blame the world!

CLAIRE. Amy, we've been together for like six months, but we're the only ones who know it.

AMY. Seven months.

CLAIRE. Don't even pull that! I thought we'd be out by now.

AMY. Claire. You know I want to, but it's just so hard with my parents.

CLAIRE. Amy, your parents don't go to this school.

AMY. Everyone else does and they mostly suck. You've seen how people treat Jenn and Michelle.

CLAIRE. It's not that bad.

AMY. Someone left a dead squirrel in Jenn's locker! How is that not bad?

CLAIRE. They laughed it off.

AMY. Because they had to! What other choice is there? It's scary – if someone could kill a squirrel and leave it, what else could they do?

CLAIRE. People are too chicken shit to do anything else. Amy, being out is not a big deal / anymore –

AMY. Of course it's a big deal! It's a big deal to me. Can't we just be left alone? No one has to know but us.

CLAIRE. Honesty is the best policy.

AMY. Oh my god! That is so lame / Claire.

CLAIRE. Whatever, I want people to know. Even just a few people at first.

AMY. If you tell Tim – I don't know. What if he gets upset and doesn't want to be your friend anymore?

CLAIRE. You didn't see his face. He was crushed. If I tell him why I really can't go to the prom with him he'll understand. I mean, he's been my friend since we were kids, our parents were divorced around the same time – his dad and my mom almost got married for God's sake!

AMY. Too bad they didn't.

CLAIRE. It would've been a tragedy! Tim's dad is such a dick.

AMY. Ha! That bumper sticker:

AMY & CLAIRE. "My other auto is a 9mm."

    (They laugh.)

CLAIRE. I feel like I owe it to him. It took a lot of guts to ask me out.

AMY. I don't know.

CLAIRE. It's not even that big of a step if we only tell him, plus – do you want to?

AMY. I told you, I don't know / Claire. I have –

CLAIRE. No I mean – ohmigod don't make me do this.

> (**CLAIRE** *kneels.*)

AMY. What are you doing? Oh no, what / are you doing?

CLAIRE. I'm so scared of you –

AMY. Oh god –

CLAIRE. Knock it off! I'm scared of you and how you really feel and what you'll really say and I mean even right now I'm getting a little sick to my stomach, but with all of this Tim stuff happening I realized that I haven't actually asked you to the stupid prom.

AMY. Ohmigod Claire –

CLAIRE. Will you go to the stupid prom with me?

> (*They let all of this sink in.*)

AMY. I'm scared too.

CLAIRE. I know.

AMY. I have another year here.

CLAIRE. I know that too.

AMY. Claire, why are you doing this to me? I can't even deal at all – and you're right, but you're also wrong. I mean okay, you make me feel amazing and happy and sad and terrible and triumphant and so angry at everything. Why the prom?! Who are we even? Okay, it's this – this is what I want to say: if I could just keep you – right here –

> (**AMY**'s *hands are balled into her chest.*)

Just right here and hold on and close my eyes I can feel so much and it's enough.

CLAIRE. I know, I know and I feel it too and it's nice. But look out there, it's so big. What if that "me and you" you keep there? What if it was out there? Everywhere.

AMY. It's so much. Ugh. I'm so stupid.

CLAIRE. Holy shit. That's your yes, isn't it?

> (**AMY** *nods.*)

Oh god, I thought you'd say no. Okay! It's too big! You're right!

AMY. No, no – no take backs. We jump in together.

CLAIRE. We're going to the prom!

> (*They celebrate and collapse into each other.*)

AMY. I'm so happy, I shouldn't be this happy!

CLAIRE. Okay, okay – and we'll start small. We'll start with Tim?

AMY. Okay, but will he even believe us?

CLAIRE. I thought of that. We'll probably have to make out for him.

AMY. Claire!

CLAIRE. I can just see the look on his face.

AMY. In that case, maybe we should start with the making out and pretend he caught us.

> (*They set the scene and then:*)

CLAIRE. Oh! Tim! Oh my god it's not what it looks like!

AMY. No, Claire. We can tell him. Tim, it *is* what it looks like.

CLAIRE. Now you know. But you can't tell anyone!

AMY. We're major lesbos Tim and we're crashing the prom, but it has to be our secret!

CLAIRE. I hope you understand now why I had to say no.

AMY. Now could you close the door real quick? We're super busy.

(*They laugh and kiss.*)

CLAIRE. Hey.

AMY. Hey.

CLAIRE. I'm glad you came up here, even though you hate it.

AMY. Where you go, I go.

CLAIRE. Look! We're on the roof! We're above everyone!

AMY. I'm going to the prom with a senior!!

(*They are over the moon laughing and happy. This was the resolution to their first fight. How nice when we realize we can move past those things.*)

5

The day of

(Classroom.)

*(****KYLE**** enters the room.)*

(He motions to the hallway and **HELEN** *enters.)*

KYLE. See? I told you this was the free period. It's like having the place to ourselves.

HELEN. I don't know, what if we get caught?

KYLE. Then we get caught. But until then, we can do whatever we want.

HELEN. And what would that be?

KYLE. Let's turn out the lights.

(He hits the switch. They embrace. As they almost kiss:)

HELEN. Wait. I just felt something.

KYLE. Yeah, I know.

Did you feel it again?

HELEN. No. Not that. Eww.

(She pushes away.)

KYLE. It's just natural.

HELEN. Wait. Here.

(She goes to a desk and sits on top of it.)

KYLE. What are you doing?

HELEN. Try this.

KYLE. Kinky.

(He goes to her desk to try to kiss her.)

HELEN. No. Get your own desk!

KYLE. But if I'm over there –

HELEN. Sit on a desk and close your eyes.

KYLE. Helen, free period ends soon –

HELEN. Kyle, please – for me?

(He tries it. They sit for a moment facing the audience.)

Do you feel anything?

KYLE. Yeah. Opportunity passing by.

HELEN. Try harder.

*(Pause. **KYLE** stands on his desk, eyes still closed. **HELEN** stands on her desk.)*

KYLE. Did you ever see that movie?

HELEN. Shh!

KYLE. Jeez.

(Pause.)

*(**CLAIRE** enters from the window and during the following tries to sneak behind them and out of the classroom.)*

HELEN. What are you thinking about?

KYLE. That movie. You know it'll drive me crazy until I remember the name of it.

HELEN. Okay, then how do you feel?

KYLE. Kinda light.

HELEN. Yeah. Light.

KYLE. Oh! The lights are off.

HELEN. There's no noise right now.

KYLE. Wow. There's usually like, a constant buzzing, right?

HELEN. Yeah, without the noise I feel…weightless.

KYLE. Why do they even use fluorescent lights?

HELEN. It's probably cheap.

KYLE. Yeah. It always comes down to money.

HELEN. I hate school.

(**CLAIRE** *decides to creep over to Mr. Y's desk.*)

KYLE. Oh my god. Did Helen Kitson just say she hates school?

HELEN. I didn't know I hated this room before right now. It's the control – it leads to stuff like this! – like sneaking around. The lights control us I think – and the inherited memories – maybe it's the old-fashioned ideas of the past. These talking walls and dusty notions – how are things ever to change? But without the lights, and without the teachers, and without the books: I can change, I can love this room!

KYLE. We have power over this room! It can do us no harm!

HELEN. There are no grades.

KYLE. No pressure.

HELEN. No humming lights.

(*They begin to hum like the fluorescent lights and the sound is not unlike bees.*)

(**CLAIRE** *can barely control her laughter.*)

CLAIRE. Hey, what's going on here?!

(**HELEN** *and* **KYLE** *are jolted and almost fall.*)

KYLE. Oh my god, Claire! You could've killed us!

HELEN. Where did you come from?

CLAIRE. I have descended from heaven to warn you free period is over soon and Mr. Y will be back to spew forth boredom.

HELEN. Oh.

CLAIRE. He comes back early.

HELEN. / Okay.

KYLE. We were just – talking.

HELEN. That's right, talking.

CLAIRE. Whatever. I don't care. Congratulations. It's fucking cute.

KYLE. You don't have to swear.

CLAIRE. Oh, grow / up.

HELEN. This is not a cute thing. We are not a cute thing.

KYLE. Hey! I'm a cute thing.

CLAIRE. Seriously, I get it. I won't tell anyone. So, you're dating, what's the big deal?

HELEN. It's a big deal to me.

KYLE. She likes keeping secrets.

HELEN. I do not!

KYLE. She finds it exciting.

HELEN. I do not!

KYLE. We both find it exciting.

CLAIRE. Secrets are exciting at first – but then they're shitty, kids. Take my word for it.

HELEN. Kyle, don't assume things about me.

KYLE. Even Claire thinks we should tell people.

CLAIRE. What do you think will happen?

KYLE. She would have to stop being nerdy and start being popular like me.

HELEN. Oh, really?

KYLE. Yeah, but it's okay. You can still be nerdy. I'm fine with it.

HELEN. Other girls like you, and I don't want to be hated.

KYLE. Who likes me?

HELEN. Um...Maria?!

KYLE. No, we grew up together.

CLAIRE. Oh, I've seen you talking to Maria –

KYLE. Stop that, we're just friends.

HELEN. She already hates me because you and I spend time together.

KYLE. Who cares?

CLAIRE. Seriously, nobody really cares. Just grow up and stop being stupid juniors. I had to be honest with someone yesterday and it sucked, but it's over and it's probably gonna get better. What is the big deal around here with not telling the truth?

KYLE. Yeah, what she said.

HELEN. Look, it's because of me, alright? I don't want anyone to know yet.

CLAIRE. Sneaking around in dark classrooms is probably not the best plan.

HELEN. It was his idea.

CLAIRE. I'm sure it was. He's obviously a pervert. Well, feel free to continue if you want Mr. Y to catch you.

(**CLAIRE** *starts to go out the door.*)

Oh my god, he's coming.

HELEN. Oh no! What do we do? Hide?

KYLE. No. Let's do the desk thing.

CLAIRE. Yeah! Back on the desks!

(*They stand on the desks and hum.*)

(**MR. Y** *enters.*)

MR. Y. We need better security in this building.

(*He hits the lights. The* **STUDENTS** *groan.*)

KYLE. That is / painful.

CLAIRE. Mr. Y. turn / them back off!

HELEN. I told you, the lights are a tool to keep us down.

MR. Y. Very funny. And now you should all get down.

(*They do.* **JAMIE J** *enters unseen and heads to the window.*)

HELEN. Sorry Mr. Y, we were doing an experiment.

MR. Y. I'm sure.

KYLE. We also wanted a reminder of what chapters to read for homework?

MR. Y. You're reading the *Iliad*, right?

CLAIRE. No, that's the Senior class.

HELEN. *Ethan Frome.*

MR. Y. Just read past Chapter Eight. Before Ethan comes to take Mattie to the train station.

KYLE. Could we read the *Iliad* instead?

CLAIRE. Be careful what you wish for.

KYLE. At least there'd be action scenes.

MR. Y. We're getting to the action scenes in *Ethan Frome.*

KYLE. Really?

CLAIRE. Yeah, some high-action sledding!

KYLE. What? No, Mr. Y!

MR. Y. It'll be great Kyle, you'll see. Now if your experiment is finished, I have to prepare for class.

CLAIRE. Oh, Mr. Y? Could we use your room to interview Mrs. Y today for the faculty portrait?

MR. Y. Why not just use her room?

CLAIRE. FBLA uses it.

MR. Y. Right. Sure, but we have a meeting right after school so you might have to wait a while.

CLAIRE. A meeting?

MR. Y. It's a little celebration for Mr. Doc's retirement.

CLAIRE. Oh, I didn't know! I can wait a little. Helen, Tim's out sick today so you're doing photos.

HELEN. Okay.

KYLE. No. I thought we were gonna do something.

HELEN. Please, you just want me to go to your game.

(As they leave:)

KYLE. Der, I need to show you my skills. Claire, you should all skip this stupid interview and come too!

CLAIRE. Nice try, pervert.

(They are gone.)

MR. Y. Jamie, are you meeting Mrs. Y tomorrow?

JAMIE J. One o'clock. Could you ask her if I should bring the big GED book?

MR. Y. Sure, and could you move it to two? I'm taking her out to Saturday brunch for her birthday and I don't want to rush.

JAMIE J. Sure thing.

MR. Y. Thanks Jamie, and good luck next week on the test.

JAMIE J. Thanks.

*(**JAMIE J** starts to leave. She turns back.)*

Mr. Y?

MR. Y. Yeah, Jamie?

JAMIE J. Should I read the *Iliad*?

MR. Y. Well, it's Mrs. Y's favorite, but I'm more partial to *Ethan Frome*. Here, I have an extra.

(He hands her the book.)

JAMIE J. Thanks. For everything.

(She is gone.)

6

A year later

(*Classroom.*)

(*During the following scene,* **JAMIE J** *tries to open the stuck window with a crowbar and she's able to budge it a little.*)

(**HELEN, MR. Y,** *and* **KYLE** *as before.* **AMY** *has started taking pictures of* **MR. Y.**)

HELEN. Question Seven: Which year was your favorite class?

MR. Y. This year.

HELEN. Everyone always says that. It doesn't have to be this year.

MR. Y. It is. What's the next question?

KYLE. How could last year not be your favorite class?! Of course it was because it has to be. Plus, graduation was sick! The whole world was here.

MR. Y. I wasn't here.

(**AMY** *starts taking close-up shots of* **MR. Y.**)

KYLE. / Oh yeah.

HELEN. Could you just mind your own business and let Mr. Y answer the questions? I'm sorry Mr. Y, we should've / been done already.

KYLE. It's not my fault, you could've rescheduled. It's very selfish.

HELEN. Selfish?! Look who's talking. This is all because I broke up with you. Well / get over it.

KYLE. Whoa there! I broke up with you.

HELEN. Kyle! Oh my god! You're out of your mind.

KYLE. I've got the text right here!

(He starts to scroll messages.)

HELEN. I never got a text! Wait, A TEXT?! That's what you think of me? At least I wrote you that long letter – you didn't read it, did you?

MR. Y. Could we / just finish?

KYLE. I don't remember any letter. Here. Here's what I wrote and it talks all about how selfish you are.

HELEN. This is ridiculous, I never got that. Plus, is it selfish to want you all to myself / to pay attention to me?

KYLE. Yes, actually that's a good definition!

MR. Y. Children / please –

HELEN. Instead of booking yourself on every talk show?

KYLE. Ah ha! Jealousy!

HELEN. Attacking the world! And I needed you and you were gone!

KYLE. No one else said shit! If not me, then who?

HELEN. They used you and you used them.

KYLE. Well – how about you, right now? This stupid interview.

HELEN. What? He's the faculty portrait! It's my job!

KYLE. But you insisted Mr. Y be the portrait – selfishly – so you could talk to him about last year! / How is it any different from what I did?

MR. Y. Kyle that's enough.

HELEN. You were after sensationalism and I'm after humanity!

KYLE. You want to interview Mr. Y for the tragedy. You just can't resist the drama.

> (**AMY** *notices* **JAMIE J** *budging the window
> and turns her attention to her.*)

AMY. Jamie...?

HELEN. This is so untrue, stop it!

KYLE. So much worse than what I did. Helen interviews
Mr. Y! His first interview since... / since last year!

HELEN. / Please, stop.

MR. Y. Kyle that really is enough.

KYLE. Mr. Y, they caught you stone-faced across the street
and asked you all those questions you weren't ready for
and that picture of you was everywhere –

AMY. Jamie...?

KYLE. "The complacent lack of grief." I got out there and
tried to fight for you... for everyone! Even in the face of
death threats – someone shot a friggin' bullet into my
house!

HELEN. I didn't / know that.

KYLE. You say you needed me well I needed you –
I couldn't keep it up. And you don't see it, but you're
solidly one of them now and bringing Amy in here is
the icing. Just using tragedy.

HELEN. I'm not! I promise / I'm not! Kyle why are you
doing this?

MR. Y. Kyle you can go, your / detention is over.

KYLE. I know because I did the same! And you were right
then, but here you are a year later... I'm trying to tell
you that nothing helps! It's not helpful to sensationalize
or mediatize or push a "one year later" section / of the
yearbook! This is her big idea, Mr. Y!

HELEN. I'm not sensationalizing, I promise Mr. Y!

MR. Y. I don't care Kyle, and I / have no objections Helen.

KYLE. You should most / definitely care, Mr. Y!

HELEN. Just fucking leave! He told you / to go! So do what you're told and leave everyone alone for once!

KYLE. Fucking leave? Nice! / Where's her detention Mr. Y?

MR. Y. I'll leave, I don't want to / be here.

AMY. *JAMIE* WHAT THE FUCK ARE YOU DOING?!

> *(Everything stops.)*

> *(**AMY** has moved so that she is halfway between **JAMIE J** and the rest of the group.)*

> *(They all look at **JAMIE J** trying to open the window. She removes her earbuds.)*

JAMIE J. I'm fixing this window, it's the / only way to reach the nest.

AMY. Why are you cleaning it first?

MR. Y. Amy.

JAMIE J. I'm not, I'm trying to scrape the paint off. I think it was painted shut –

AMY. That's bullshit. It's not paint is it?

JAMIE J. Of course it is. What else would it be?

> *(**JAMIE J** shows a rag to point out the paint, but it definitely looks suspicious. **JAMIE J** hides the rag.)*

AMY. I don't know –

MR. Y. Amy, maybe you have enough pictures.

JAMIE J. It's been stuck a long time – at least before –

AMY. Before –?

JAMIE J. It would've been painted shut a long time ago.

AMY. But, this is where it happened so it could be… couldn't it? I mean, I don't know I just see the mess… and it looks like… I don't know… my god, we're standing in a fucking graveyard.

> (**AMY** *looks over to the tape recorder. She grabs it and runs out of the room.*)

HELEN. Amy?

MR. Y. Sit tight, everyone.

> (**MR. Y** *follows* **AMY**.)

> (**JAMIE J** *goes out the open window.*)

> (**KYLE** *sits pathetically.*)

KYLE. This is why Helen. This is why you shouldn't – you just shouldn't ever, especially not in this room.

> (**HELEN** *goes to him.*)

This fucking room.

7

The day of

(Classroom.)

*(**AMY, CLAIRE** with a notepad.)*

*(**HELEN** struggling to change film in the camera.)*

AMY. How long is this retirement celebration supposed to be?

CLAIRE. It can't be too long.

AMY. You should just make Mr. Doc the faculty portrait.

CLAIRE. They use him like, every four years or so.

AMY. But he's interesting, he's been here forever, and this is his last year.

CLAIRE. Mrs. Y's been here for twenty years and she's plenty interesting.

AMY. Then why did she marry Mr. Y?

CLAIRE. That's one of my questions:

*(Grabs recorder and holds mic to **AMY**.)*

Mrs. Y, why did you marry Mr. Y?

AMY. So I could fall asleep at night to his boring voice.

HELEN. Amy!

AMY. What? He's boring.

HELEN. I don't think so.

CLAIRE. He's alright, but his classes are definitely boring, why do you think he's never been the faculty portrait?

HELEN. He could totally be the faculty portrait.

AMY. Ugh.

CLAIRE. Not on my watch. Mrs. Y is so much more interesting.

HELEN. I know, but maybe Mr. Y could do it next year.

AMY. I'll be head writer next year, thank you, and there is NO WAY that Mr. Y is F.P.

HELEN. We'll see.

AMY. We *will* see, camera girl.

CLAIRE. Do you know how to use that thing?

HELEN. I've only replaced rolls a couple of times. Of all days, why is Tim sick today?

   *(**AMY** looks at **CLAIRE** guiltily.)*

AMY. A more important question is why don't we have frigging digital cameras?

CLAIRE. Because the darkroom is so cool.

HELEN. Totally. Ah! I think I got it. *(She closes the back of the camera and listens.)* Nope.

CLAIRE. Stupid juniors.

AMY. Hey! I'm a junior!

CLAIRE. Um, yeah!

AMY. You must like hanging out with morons.

CLAIRE. Well when that's all there are –

AMY. Nice.

HELEN. Get a room.

CLAIRE & AMY. What?

HELEN. What?

AMY. Why did you say that?

HELEN. Jeez, it's a joke. Lighten up.

CLAIRE. Oh.

> (**CLAIRE** *nods her head toward* **HELEN** *á la:*
> *"Let's tell her." **AMY** shakes her head "no.")*

AMY. Maybe we should give up.

HELEN. Okay.

CLAIRE. Are you kidding? We're already here and she has
to be done with the meeting soon.

AMY. I have to be home for Stevie.

CLAIRE. He's like twelve, he'll be fine.

AMY. If I'm not there he eats a bunch of sweets, or worse
his signature peanut butter and mayonnaise sandwich.

HELEN. Oh / gross!

CLAIRE. Sick!

AMY. And he gets mayo all in the PB and vice versa and
Mom's like: "Where were you?" and it's a huge pain in
the ass, so I'm giving Mrs. Y five more minutes.

CLAIRE. Amy, just stay!

HELEN. Yeah, and I want to go check out the baseball game.

CLAIRE. Come on, Helen!

HELEN. We can take her picture any time.

CLAIRE. But we have a deadline, and it's always a picture
at the time of the interview! How are you two supposed
to learn how to do the faculty portrait if we don't do it
right!

AMY. Um, you just told us what to do? Also, we could fake
the photo another time.

CLAIRE. We will not break tradition. It's not my fault
Stevie's a disgusting little shit.

AMY. Hey, that's my brother.

CLAIRE. I've got a little brother AND a little sister and they're ten and eight and they're fine by themselves.

AMY. They just sit around and watch TV!

CLAIRE. So?

AMY. They're robots! I've never seen any family so devoid of emotion. The whole bunch of you need a cattle prod or something!

CLAIRE. You should talk.

AMY. At least my family likes me.

CLAIRE. Oh my god!

HELEN. Get a room.

   (Pause. Then they all laugh.)

AMY. Textbook Helen.

CLAIRE. Fine. Five minutes. Then you can both leave, but I *will* get this interview today. Just give me the stupid camera.

   (She begins to put the roll in correctly.)

HELEN. I knew she'd do it eventually.

AMY. She's the most stubborn person I know. But we'll get her to leave with us –

CLAIRE. We'll see.

AMY. We *will* see.

CLAIRE. Stupid juniors.

   (She closes the camera and presents it to **HELEN.**)

So easy.

8

A year later

(The hallway.)

*(**JAMIE J** spot sweeping with earbuds in.)*

*(**KYLE** comes around the corner unseen and heads to Mr. Y's room. He's drawn to **JAMIE J** and starts in her direction. **JAMIE J** senses him as he gets close and turns. They both jump.)*

KYLE. Sorry Jamie, I scare ya?

JAMIE J. Did you do that on purpose?

KYLE. No.

JAMIE J. You should be more careful.

KYLE. Yeah, I'm hearing that. Makes you feel more alive though, right?

JAMIE J. Wrong.

> *(**JAMIE J** returns to sweeping. **KYLE** taps her. She jumps.)*

Oh my god!

KYLE. Jamie J, how much you get paid?

JAMIE J. What?! I don't know.

KYLE. You don't know?

JAMIE J. Or I don't want to tell you.

KYLE. I guess you can't put a price on it.

JAMIE J. I didn't say that, they definitely put a price on it.

KYLE. Is it worth it?

JAMIE J. Don't you got somewhere to be?

KYLE. It's embarrassing. I snapped Maria's bra strap in Mr. Y's class and he's making me stay after. But he doesn't know, you know, she's like my best friend since I was two, she likes it.

JAMIE J. She said she likes having her bra snapped?

KYLE. Well, she called me a pervert.

JAMIE J. That's not really the same thing.

KYLE. No. I guess it isn't, but – I didn't mean nothing by it, you know?

JAMIE J. Said the future rapist –

KYLE. Yikes! Jamie!

JAMIE J. It sounds to me like you should respect people more, Mr. Television.

KYLE. Okay, it was wrong and I was wrong and I'm a total asshole alright! It just sucks to stay after and miss practice – especially in that room.

JAMIE J. Why does he still teach in there anyway? They should've torn this whole place down.

KYLE. Wow, hot take – anyway, JJ could you do me a favor and pop into Mr. Y's room and entertain me?

JAMIE J. Now why would I do that?

KYLE. Look, I'm sorry JJ for scaring you and stuff, I'm only messing around. But you're the only one who can help me. All he's gonna do is make me sit there and read the *Iliad* and I already read the damn thing.

JAMIE J. Do you deserve it?

KYLE. I don't deserve anything.

JAMIE J. At least you're honest. Listen, no promises because I got stuff to do, but maybe I could finally get that hornet's nest down.

KYLE. That sounds important.

JAMIE J. I thought the winter would kill 'em, but they're tough little buggers. Now the nest is pretty big.

KYLE. Don't forget, okay? I owe you one.

(He turns to go.)

JAMIE J. Kyle –

KYLE. Yeah?

JAMIE J. I... I haven't been in there since –

KYLE. Oh. But you stayed at the school for a reason right? Maybe this is it.

JAMIE J. Don't push it.

*(**KYLE** goes into class. **JAMIE J** leaves.)*

9

The day of

(Darkroom. Very red. A few pictures hanging.
AMY *enters.)*

CLAIRE. Don't touch the light, I'm still drying!

AMY. Fine, but we should hurry. Helen's probably waiting
for Mrs. Y already.

CLAIRE. I know, but I just need a sec – plus I'm getting her
the camera.

AMY. Why didn't she get it?

CLAIRE. She forgot.

AMY & CLAIRE. Textbook Helen.

*(**CLAIRE** grabs the camera from a shelf.)*

AMY. So, Tim's out sick, hunh?

CLAIRE. Yeah. He took it hard. But, how are you doing?

AMY. I'm okay.

CLAIRE. Really?

AMY. Yeah, I mean don't throw a parade or anything –

CLAIRE. Oh my god! I told you, it's okay and you shouldn't
worry.

AMY. I guess.

CLAIRE. As far as I'm concerned, the problem is solved.

AMY. I wouldn't go that far.

CLAIRE. I would! This is just the beginning.

AMY. Maybe that's the problem. I was fine all day around other people, but now that we're alone, I'm the friggin' drama club.

CLAIRE. Well I'm super sorry. Get over it – just for that, you carry the camera.

> (*She hands it to her.* **HELEN** *enters* **A year later**.)

HELEN. Amy?

> (**CLAIRE** *takes her dry photos down.*)

AMY. I can't help how I feel.

HELEN. You can still back out if you want to.

AMY. Am I making this harder than it really is?

HELEN. It's not a big deal.

CLAIRE. Of course, but only because it's important now. It means something.

HELEN. I could take pictures separately – I'm sure Mr. Y wouldn't mind.

AMY. Yeah. Maybe.

CLAIRE. Now put your public face on and let's get rolling. Don't forget the tape recorder.

> (**CLAIRE** *leaves.*)

> (**AMY** *picks up the tape recorder.*)

HELEN. There's no reason to force anything.

AMY. I want to try.

HELEN. I know, but –

AMY. It's okay. I need to do this.

> (**AMY** *turns to* **HELEN** *and shows her the tape recorder.*)

HELEN. Amy! You found the tape recorder! Where was it?

AMY. Buried.

HELEN. I've looked for this all year.

AMY. Two months ago – a box showed up in here. Someone put it out of the way, I don't think it was meant to be noticed or even opened.

HELEN. Oh.

AMY. Kinda wish I never opened it.

> (**HELEN** *hands back the recorder.*)

HELEN. Bring it, it'll make the interview easier – I write slow as molasses. We should get going. We'll be late.

AMY. I'll be right there.

HELEN. Okay.

> (**HELEN** *leaves.*)

> (**AMY** *sits as the scene shifts to:*)

10

(Roof.)

(**AMY** *pulling the film from the camera, exposing it to the sun.*)

(**MR. Y** *pulls himself up.*)

MR. Y. It's easier to get up here than I thought.

AMY. …

MR. Y. Good view.

AMY. …

MR. Y.
   "IS YOUR VISION CLEAR?" *

AMY. …

MR. Y. You come up here a lot?

AMY. …

MR. Y. Listen, Amy. You know and I know there's nothing
   – no right word, no action – but please know we're
   all dealing with the same thing. Different sides of the
   same problem. Like the blind people and the elephant.

   (She stops unspooling.)

AMY. Mr. Y? What the hell are you talking about?

MR. Y. You've never heard that story?

AMY. Nope.

MR. Y. Well, these blind people touch different parts of
   an elephant and then describe what they're touching.
   But the animal is so big they all come to different
   conclusions and start arguing – no one backs down,

---

* Sheet music for "Vision" is included at the end of this volume.

the tension heightens – the point is: in the end, they're all correct in their descriptions, but since everything is subjective, they don't take the time to talk to each other and figure it out.

AMY. How do they find out it's an elephant?

MR. Y. Oh, I don't remember –

MR. Y & AMY. Maybe they never do.

> *(They chuckle at this overlap.)*

AMY. Mr. Y – I can't accept they've been gone for a year – Principal Mays, Claire, Mrs. Y – it seems like yesterday they were here.

MR. Y. Yeah. And a million years ago. You know – this is so stupid – last night I was doing laundry and one of Mrs. Y's socks came out of the dryer. It must've been stuck in a sheet or something. I still have her dresser – couldn't part with it, in fact it's full of clothes – it's one of those tall dark stained antique dressers, little keyholes – I opened the drawer to put the sock in and – exhaustion overtook me. I went over to the bed, got under the covers – fully clothed – and curled up with the sock. Best night I've had for a while.

AMY. Do you think the matching sock was in the drawer?

MR. Y. I don't want to find out. There's a finality involved, almost as if I complete the pair my memories would dissipate or something.

AMY. I don't think the memories'll ever go away.

MR. Y. Yeah –

> *(He pulls the sock out of his pocket.)*

But just in case, you know?

AMY. Just in case.

MR. Y. Do you have anything from Claire?

AMY. ...?

MR. Y. It's okay, I know.

AMY. Mr. Y. You know? About me and Claire? Does everyone know?

MR. Y. What do you think?

AMY. I don't know because – no one ever talked to me about it. No one has said a word to me about her. But they avoid me. And I let them. I was in love Mr. Y, and I wouldn't let Claire tell anyone because I was scared – and then we did – and the exact worst thing happened. And it's my fault; if I wasn't afraid from the beginning and we were open – and that day Mrs. Y, I'm so sorry – maybe I'd be up here with Claire right now and you'd be heading home to your wife.

MR. Y. Amy, there's a short list of people to blame and you're not on it. This is the fault of one person – and let me tell you something – don't think for a second this school building is not full of people with deep guilt and hurt to rival our own. We stuck around and now we're trapped in this building – the reminders all around us – and the only thing we have is each other. In a way, we're lucky that there are people who suffer every day just as much as we do. In fact, it's dangerous not to remember that. It's the best memorial.

AMY. I do have one thing –

> (**AMY** *flips the tape over and presses play on the recorder. From the small speakers:*)

VOICE OF CLAIRE. *Testing...testing. I think it's good. There are eight questions, Mrs. Y –*

VOICE OF MRS. Y. *I know. Ugh, I can't believe he teaches in this room.*

MR. Y. Oh my god.

> (**AMY** *rises and stands on the edge of the roof.*)

VOICE OF CLAIRE.

I know, it just adds to the snooze-fest. Question One: When did you start here?

VOICE OF MRS. Y.

Twenty years ago, the year before Mr. Y.

VOICE OF CLAIRE.

Question Two: What was your first day like?

VOICE OF MRS. Y.

I was a little lost, but I've always been good with new people and settled in quickly. I remember thinking I could teach here forever.

VOICE OF CLAIRE.

Forever?

VOICE OF MRS. Y.

Is that question three?

AMY.

I told her once that I could jump, but I was lying, I never would've done it. But now I can imagine it and it wouldn't even hurt.

MR. Y.

It would hurt quite a bit actually.

AMY.

It's only two stories.

MR. Y.

We'd have to land on our heads.

AMY.

We?

(**MR. Y** *offers the sock.*)

(**AMY** *takes the end of it.*)

(*They close their eyes for a moment.*)

(*From the tape:*)

VOICE OF CLAIRE. *No. Question Three is a fluff question: What's your favorite song?*

VOICE OF MRS. Y. *That's easy, "Vision" by Barnaby.*

VOICE OF CLAIRE. *What's that?*

VOICE OF MRS. Y. *You've never heard it?*

VOICE OF CLAIRE. *Nope.*

VOICE OF MRS. Y.
   "IS YOUR VISION CLEAR?
   IS YOUR VISION BLURRY?"

VOICE OF CLAIRE. *Not ringing any / bells – I'll take your word for it.*

   (Instead of jumping, **MR. Y** *lets* **AMY** *hold the sock.)*

AMY. It's soft.

   (**MR. Y** *turns off the tape.*)

MR. Y. Does this tape go – all the way to – the end?

AMY. No – god no! It's just the interview. They finished – they were done.

MR. Y. Okay. Did I ever tell you about when I met Mrs. Y?

AMY. No.

MR. Y. I used to tell all my classes, but eventually they stopped being interested…or I did.

AMY. Was it like Principal Doc's story?

MR. Y. No, but it did happen on my first day. I took her parking space. There's this moment in daily life I like to call the impulse point; the point where you could make a nice and compassionate choice over the jerk choice. It happens a lot to me when I'm driving. Running red lights, tailgating, cutting people off, flipping people off –

AMY. Mr. Y, you drive like a badass!

MR. Y. Mrs. Y said it was my Achilles' heel. This parking spot was like an oasis and I saw another car that might've had the priority. Instead of backing off, I crossed the impulse point and hit the gas. So I'm sitting in the car waiting for the other car to move on. It doesn't. In fact, the car pulls up behind me and blocks me in. I slowly peek out the window and there she is, with this look on her face that wasn't the road rage I expected, but more of a compassionate "I feel sorry for you" type of look. I made it my life's mission to change that look on her face to one of admiration.

AMY. How long did that take?

MR. Y. Eight years.

AMY. Oh my god. I wish I'd had eight years with Claire.

MR. Y. I wish I had eight more.

AMY. I wish I had eight hundred more.

MR. Y. Eight thousand.

AMY. I'd settle for eight minutes.

Thanks for coming after me.

MR. Y. It's nice up here, and I'm sure it helps, but it's also lonely.

AMY. I'm okay with lonely. Every once in a while.

(She offers the sock to **MR. Y.** *He takes it.)*

(He makes to throw it off the roof, baseball-style.)

NO! Mr. Y don't!

(He pulls the sock back in.)

MR. Y. We don't need these things Amy. You should toss that tape.

(**AMY** *removes the tape from the recorder.
They consider tossing the items off the edge.*)

AMY. Maybe we could just trade? I mean, not because we
need to, but because if we throw these off the roof, it
would be littering.

(*He laughs and they trade.*)

MR. Y. Yeah. Okay.

Well, what do you say we go send everyone home?

AMY. Deal.

(*She grabs the camera and the exposed film.*)

11

(Meanwhile...)

(Classroom.)

*(**HELEN** and **KYLE** are seated next to each other, holding hands a little.)*

KYLE. You know, technically we never broke up.

HELEN. What?

KYLE. I mean, if you didn't read my text and I didn't read your letter –

HELEN. So, like the last year didn't happen?

KYLE. Sorta like that.

HELEN. But it did happen.

KYLE. I was thinking like, it's never too late. Sometimes when we try to help other people, we forget about ourselves.

HELEN. And sometimes when we try to help ourselves we forget about other people.

*(They kiss. **JAMIE J** looks through the window.)*

JAMIE J. Get a room.

*(They separate. **JAMIE J** enters cigs first.)*

HELEN. Oh! Hi, JJ! Were you just smoking?

JAMIE J. Yeah.

HELEN. It's really bad for you.

JAMIE J. Yeah.

KYLE. What kind you got?

HELEN. Kyle!

KYLE. Just curious.

JAMIE J. The cheapest kind.

KYLE. Oh. I prefer Camels.

JAMIE J. Me too. You wanna bum one?

HELEN. Kyle.

KYLE. Relax Mom, it's baseball season. Maybe next time.

> (**JAMIE J** *goes back to scraping.* **AMY** *and* **MR. Y** *enter.)*

Hey guys. Sorry we were fighting.

HELEN. Yeah – so unnecessary.

AMY. Don't sweat it.

MR. Y. Helen, do you have what you need?

HELEN. One more question: Where do you see yourself in ten years?

MR. Y. Hm. Still teaching I guess.

HELEN. Same classroom?

> (*He considers the room. Maybe he sees it differently.*)

MR. Y. You know? I don't know –

> (*Not able to ignore* **JAMIE J***'s scraping:)*

Jamie, could you do that another time?

AMY. Actually, do you mind if I help?

JAMIE J. You sure?

AMY. Yeah, I just freaked out a bit.

JAMIE J. Grab a scraper.

(She begins helping. After a moment, she sings "Vision" by Barnaby. The singing should start slowly and personally. The rest of the group also make their way to the window one at a time during the song. All save **MR. Y** *are scraping by the end. Maybe there's a rhythm.)*

AMY. *(Singing.)*
IS YOUR VISION CLEAR?
IS YOUR VISION BLURRY?
IS YOUR VISION CLEAR?
IS YOUR VISION BLURRY?

KYLE. *(Joins.)*
IS YOUR VISION CLEAR?
IS YOUR VISION BLURRY?

ALL.
IS YOUR VISION CLEAR?
IS YOUR VISION BLURRY?
IS YOUR VISION CLEAR?
IS YOUR VISION BLURRY?
IS YOUR VISION CLEAR?
IS YOUR VISION BLURRY?
IS YOUR VISION CLEAR?
IS YOUR VISION BLURRY?

*(***JAMIE J*** *gives* **MR. Y** *a look.)*

JAMIE J. Well, let's give it a go!

*(***MR. Y*** *crosses to them.)*

MR. Y. I'll try from outside.

(They all find a place to push up on the window as **MR. Y** *goes to the other side. He removes his teacher's suit jacket. As he is about to heave,* **CLAIRE** *enters the ledge area and everyone else freezes.* **MR. Y** *succumbs to memory as it shifts to:)*

12

The day before

(Outside ledge. **MR. Y** *and* **CLAIRE.***)*

CLAIRE. Oh! Mr. Y, I was just – I dropped my – class project.

MR. Y. Don't worry Claire, I know you come out here.

CLAIRE. You do? Why don't you stop me?

MR. Y. I figure you have a good reason.

CLAIRE. Not really.

MR. Y. You should think of one because I don't think a nic fit qualifies.

CLAIRE. How about general rebelliousness? Mental health break?

MR. Y. Because the world is so hard and cold?

CLAIRE. You have no idea, Mr. Y.

MR. Y. Try me.

(He sits on the ledge. She follows.)

CLAIRE. Did you ever have to keep your relationship with Mrs. Y a secret? You know, because you both work here?

MR. Y. Oh I see, forbidden love. Not a terrible reason to be out here, and you're in good company.

CLAIRE. Good company. You mean like Juliet? Like Helen of Troy? Like Mattie from *Ethan Frome*?

MR. Y. Okay, okay, I take your meaning.

CLAIRE. So did you? Have to be sneaky?

MR. Y. No, because by the time she agreed to go out with me everyone knew anyway – it was a cumulative awareness.

CLAIRE. Ha! I like that – cumulative. Where did you take her on your first date?

MR. Y. Sushi, her favorite – I asked around and found out her favorite song, scoured the record store, and when I picked her up and turned on the car, there was that "Vision" song. She flipped out.

CLAIRE. She was pissed?

MR. Y. Flipped out in a good way.

CLAIRE. The person I'm dating now likes The White Stripes. We have a song, but the middle part is "I get nervous when she comes around." Do you think that's a bad sign?

MR. Y. Depends on what kind of nervous they mean.

CLAIRE. Sure, I guess. Oh Mr. Y, do you want one of these?

MR. Y. No, I quit long ago and it shouldn't have taken so long to stop. You actually like it?

> *(Maybe during this speech, the frozen tableau in the classroom moves to a second tableau to better lift the window.)*

CLAIRE. I don't know. When I take a drag it's like I'm not so much pulling smoke in, but like I'm connecting to other moments. There's something about holding in the smoke that does something – completes a thought, or lights a memory – and it shakes me, Mr. Y. It shakes me down to the ground because I can be in all those places because of smell and taste. Almost like how they say that time doesn't really exist in a straight line, it's just piled on top of itself and branches and everything that's happened in our lives is happening at the same time. Inhaling connects me to all of those places, and when I exhale I can let them go – all of the memories.

MR. Y. Those are just tobacco, right?

CLAIRE. Shut up.

MR. Y. So if all of time is happening now, shouldn't we be able to see what happens next?

CLAIRE. Worth a shot.

> *(She takes a drag. Holds it as long as possible. She wants to see what will happen. Maybe she does. Maybe we do as well. Long exhale.)*

MR. Y. Well?

CLAIRE. I'm not gonna tell.

MR. Y. Tell me this: am I still teaching here?

CLAIRE. Still teaching, but it didn't look like here.

MR. Y. Trying to get rid of me, hunh? Did you see Mrs. Y?

CLAIRE. Nope, didn't see her.

MR. Y. She's probably President or something. You know, I stopped smoking because of Mrs. Y. She wouldn't even THINK of dating me if I didn't stop. So I quit and I made it about a year and then – I had one little cigarette – it was just a little treat, but it led to another and then another and then a whole pack.

CLAIRE. How did you hide it?

MR. Y. I had so much peppermint around you'd think it was Christmas. Of course she found out eventually and I backtracked and apologized, but she wouldn't talk to me for a month. It was the worst month ever. But my point is, she wasn't mad at me because of the smoking really, it's because I wasn't honest with her. If you can lie about one thing you can lie about anything.

CLAIRE. I see what you're doing there.

MR. Y. Honesty is the best policy.

CLAIRE. Ugh, Mr. Y, it's not that easy.

MR. Y. Why not?

CLAIRE. It's just not. Because it's not just me, there's other people involved and it's complicated and I don't know, but you know what? That's why I need to be out here!

MR. Y. Well, period's almost over so you shouldn't be out here now.

CLAIRE. You know, you're okay Mr. Y. Your lectures are still boring though / you gotta work on those.

MR. Y. Alright, let's go.

CLAIRE. To be continued Mr. Y, to be continued.

> *(She exits. **MR. Y** gets stung on the back of the neck.)*

MR. Y. Ow!

> *(He looks up and finds the nest.)*

Hunh.

> *(His attention turns to the window where everyone is still frozen. He returns to the position he was in before **CLAIRE** entered and the scene shifts to:)*

13

A year later

JAMIE J. Okay, on three. One, two, three.

(They heave and it still doesn't budge.)

MR. Y. Oh, fuck!

KYLE. Mr. Y... yes!!

MR. Y. Oh, so we've stopped singing?
IS YOUR VISION CLEAR?
IS YOUR VISION BLURRY?

(They all join and as they sing they slowly raise the window.)

ALL.
IS YOUR VISION CLEAR?
IS YOUR VISION BLURRY?
IS YOUR VISION CLEAR?
IS YOUR VISION BLURRY?
IS YOUR VISION CLEAR?
IS YOUR VISION BLURRY?

(When it is all the way up, everyone on the classroom side cheers. High fives. Hugs.)

JAMIE J. Thanks everyone!

*(After the exultation of the window repair the group takes a moment to admire the open window. Then **AMY** and **HELEN** move to pack up their stuff, **KYLE** goes to his desk and backpack, and **JAMIE J** starts to continue getting the nest.)*

> *(Just as it seems there will be nothing else said,* **MR. Y** *enters from the window and* **HELEN** *makes a decision:)*

HELEN. Mr. Y, Kyle sent me this picture he took of you earlier –?

KYLE. Helen! Mr. Y, I totally didn't mean anything / by it, I was just bored –

HELEN. Kyle, knock it off. Can I use this?

> *(She holds her phone out.)*

MR. Y. Oh. Hunh. Okay.

HELEN. Okay?

MR. Y. Okay, you can use it.

HELEN. Sweet!

KYLE. You're welcome, Helen. I'll need some credit on that.

MR. Y. I have one condition.

> *(He pulls the tape out of his pocket.)*

Could you make this year's portrait two teachers?

HELEN. Two? Is this –?

AMY. Last year is on the other side.

KYLE. Shut up.

HELEN. I don't know what to say – I mean, yes of course, but – okay, if you want me to I will because it would be so amazingly cool and touching and it could make a lot of people happy and I really think some of us deserve to be happy this year and I promise it'll just be perfect. What I mean is – I'll work really hard on it.

MR. Y. I know you will. Did we finish the faculty portrait?

HELEN. I have enough. Thanks, Mr. Y. For everything.

AMY. Yeah, thanks.

KYLE. Yeah, yeah, yeah – come on, let's go! Bye JJ!!

> (**AMY, HELEN,** *and* **KYLE** *exit.*)

JAMIE J. Well, moment of truth time.

> (**JAMIE J** *heads to the window.*)

MR. Y. Hold on a sec.

> (**MR. Y** *pulls out a pack of cigarettes.*)

> (*As* **JAMIE J** *looks at him:*)

Do you mind, JJ?

JAMIE J. Knock yourself out.

> (**MR. Y** *lights one up.*)

MR. Y. You wanna bum one?

JAMIE J. I got my own.

> (**JAMIE J** *lights one up.*)

> (**MR. Y** *crosses to the window behind* **JAMIE J.***)

MR. Y. Gotta get in the mood.

JAMIE J. Damn straight.

> (**JAMIE J** *picks up the pole and leans out of the window.*)

> (**MR. Y** *starts humming the melody to* "Vision".)

> (**JAMIE J** *deftly gives a push and a big, grey hive flies by the window and to the ground as they watch.*)

End of Play

NOTE ON STAGING

In previous productions, the hive was a physical presence above the stage (not visible to the audience) and when Mr. Y pokes the hive at the end, the object would release and fall to the stage floor with a loud thud followed by (or during) a quick blackout complete with buzzing noises of hornets escaping. The result is jarring and a very effective ending, so I highly recommend doing something similar.

Vision

Sean David DeMers

The excerpt above is from a song written specifically for this show. Please treat this as a guideline and feel free to play with different keys as needed for your cast since this will be a cappella and should feel free and imperfect.